Quentin Blake's
NURSERY RHYME BOOK

Mini Treasures

RED FOX

1 3 5 7 9 10 8 6 4 2

Illustrations © 1983 Quentin Blake

Quentin Blake has asserted his right under the Copyright,
Designs and Patents Act, 1988
to be identified as illustrator of this work

The author and publishers are grateful to Oxford University Press for
permission to use the rhymes, some from Iona and Peter Opie's Oxford
Dictionary of Nursery Rhymes (1951) and some from their
Oxford Nursery Rhyme Book (1955)

First published in the United Kingdom 1983
by Jonathan Cape
First published in Mini Treasures edition 1996
by Red Fox
Random House, 20 Vauxhall Bridge Road, London SW1V 2SA

Random House Australia (Pty) Limited
20 Alfred Street, Milsons Point, Sydney,
New South Wales 2061, Australia

Random House New Zealand Limited
18 Poland Road, Glenfield,
Auckland 10, New Zealand

Random House South Africa (Pty) Limited
PO Box 2263, Rosebank 2121, South Africa

Random House UK Limited Reg. No. 954009

A CIP catalogue record for this book
is available from the British Library

ISBN 009 9725 614

Printed in Singapore

Little Jack Sprat
  Once had a pig,
It was not very little,
  Nor yet very big,
It was not very lean,
  It was not very fat–
It's a good pig to grunt,
  Said little Jack Sprat.

OINK

Ickel ockle, blue bockle,
Fishes in the sea,

If you want a pretty maid,
Please choose me.

Jeremiah,
blow the fire,
Puff, puff, puff.

First you blow it gently

Then you blow it rough.

Handy spandy, Jack-a-Dandy
Loves plum cake and sugar candy.
He bought some at a
grocer's shop

And out he came,
hop, hop,
hop, hop!

Gregory Griggs,
Gregory Griggs,
Had twenty-seven
different wigs.

He wore them up,
he wore them down
To please the people
of the town;

He wore them east,
   he wore them west,
But he never could tell
   which he loved the best.

Dickery, dickery, dare,
 The pig flew up in the air;

The man in brown
    soon brought him down,
Dickery, dickery, dare.

I had a little husband
    No bigger than my thumb;
I put him in a pint pot
    And there I bid him drum.
I gave him some garters
    To garter up his hose,
And a little silk handkerchief
    To wipe his pretty nose.

Pussy Cat ate the dumplings,
Pussy Cat ate the dumplings,
Mama stood by,
And cried, Oh, fie!
Why did you eat
the dumplings?

William McTrimbletoe,
  He's a good fisherman,

Catches fishes

Puts them in dishes,

Catches hens
    Puts them in pens,

Some lay eggs

Some lay none

William McTrimbletoe,
He doesn't eat one.

FRESH
FISH

EGGS
FOR SALE

Pretty John Watts,
We are troubled with rats,
Will you drive them out of the house?

We have mice, too, in plenty
That feast in the pantry,
But let them stay,
And nibble away:
What harm is a little brown mouse?

Little Blue Ben,
        who lives in the glen,
Keeps a blue cat
        and one blue hen

Which lays of blue eggs
a score and ten;
Where shall I find
the little Blue Ben?

Goosey, goosey gander,
Who stands yonder?
Little Betsy Baker;

Take her up
and shake her.

Terence McDiddler,

The three-stringed fiddler,

Can charm, if you please,

The fish from the seas!

Robin the Bobbin
   the big-bellied Ben
He ate more meat
   than fourscore men.

He ate a cow
   he ate a calf
He ate a butcher
   and a half

He ate a church
  he ate a steeple
He ate a priest
  and all the people

A cow and a calf
A butcher and a half
A church and a steeple
And all the good people

And yet he complained
  that his stomach wasn't
      full.

Here am I
Little Jumping Joan;

When nobody's with me
I'm all alone.

Oh, Mother,
I shall be married
    to Mr Punchinello,

To Mr Punch,
    To Mr Joe,
        To Mr Nell,
            To Mr Lo,

Mr Punch, Mr Joe,
Mr Nell, Mr Lo,
To Mr Punchinello!